W9-BEJ-778

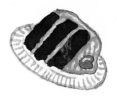

To Lonni Sue, the catalyst,
Jean, the catapult,
and Brack who, I hope,
will engineer a way to avert
real future catastrophe.

The
FAT CATS,
COUSIN SCRAGGS
and the
MONSTER MICE

by Barbara Shook Hazen
illustrated by Lonni Sue Johnson

ATHENEUM   1985   NEW YORK

Property Of
Bound Brook Schools
LAFAYETTE SCHOOL

11.95 B+t 5/7/85

BOOKS BY BARBARA SHOOK HAZEN

The Gorilla Did It
Gorilla Wants to Be the Baby
The Ups and Downs of Marvin
Why Couldn't I Be an Only Kid Like You, Wigger
Step On It, Andrew
Even If I Did Something Awful
The Fat Cats, Cousin Scraggs and the Monster Mice

BOOKS ILLUSTRATED BY LONNI SUE JOHNSON

A Snake Is Totally Tail
(Judi Barrett)
———————

The Fat Cats, Cousin Scraggs and the Monster Mice

Library of Congress Cataloging in Publication Data

Hazen, Barbara Shook,
The fat cats, cousin scraggs and the monster mice.

SUMMARY: Relates how Cousin Scraggs saves the Fat
Cat family from an attack by monster mice and eventually,
leads them to a simpler but happier life.
1. Children's stories, American.   [1. Cats—Fiction]
I. Johnson, L. S. (Lonni Sue), ill.   II. Title.
PZ7.H314975Fat   1985   [E]   84-20457
ISBN 0-689-31092-7

Text copyright © 1985 by Barbara Shook Hazen
Pictures copyright © 1985 by Lonni Sue Johnson
All rights reserved
Published simultaneously in Canada by
McClelland & Stewart, Ltd.
Text set by Linoprint Composition, New York City
Printed and bound by South China Printing Company, Hong Kong
Typography by Mary Ahern
First American Edition

Once there was a family of fat cats
who lived in a big house in great comfort
if not closeness.

They had everything to make them happy,
which was the one thing they weren't.

Father Cat had a workshop so full of fantastic gidgets

and gadgets he never had to work.

Mother Cat had a kitchen so full of fantastic appliances she never had to cook.

Indeed, she could whip up the most amazing concoctions,
like mouse moose and snail souffle, by the mere press
of a paw, while watching TV *and* having her back rubbed.

Sis Cat had her own room full of self-pampering devices, everything from fur fluffers to toenail buffers, plus a magnifying mirror in which to admire herself.

Son Cat had every electronic game ever invented, everything from Pack Rat to Star Boars, plus a Compute-a-Cat programmed to play with him but never win.

One day, into this posh and pampered
life, came Cousin Scraggs. He came with
only his wits and his whiskers and
five generations of fleas.

He came because he was hungry. The
food scraps he used to scrounge from the

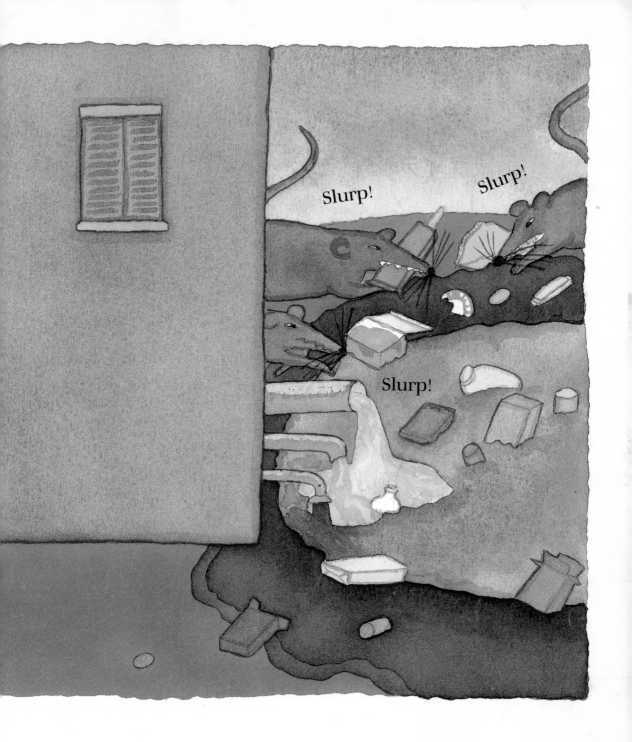

fat cats' garbage were now pulverized,
chemically pureed and poured into the fat cats' pond.

He came because he wanted to warn his
cousins about the big, mean-looking mice
who were drinking from the pond.

And he came because he was curious.

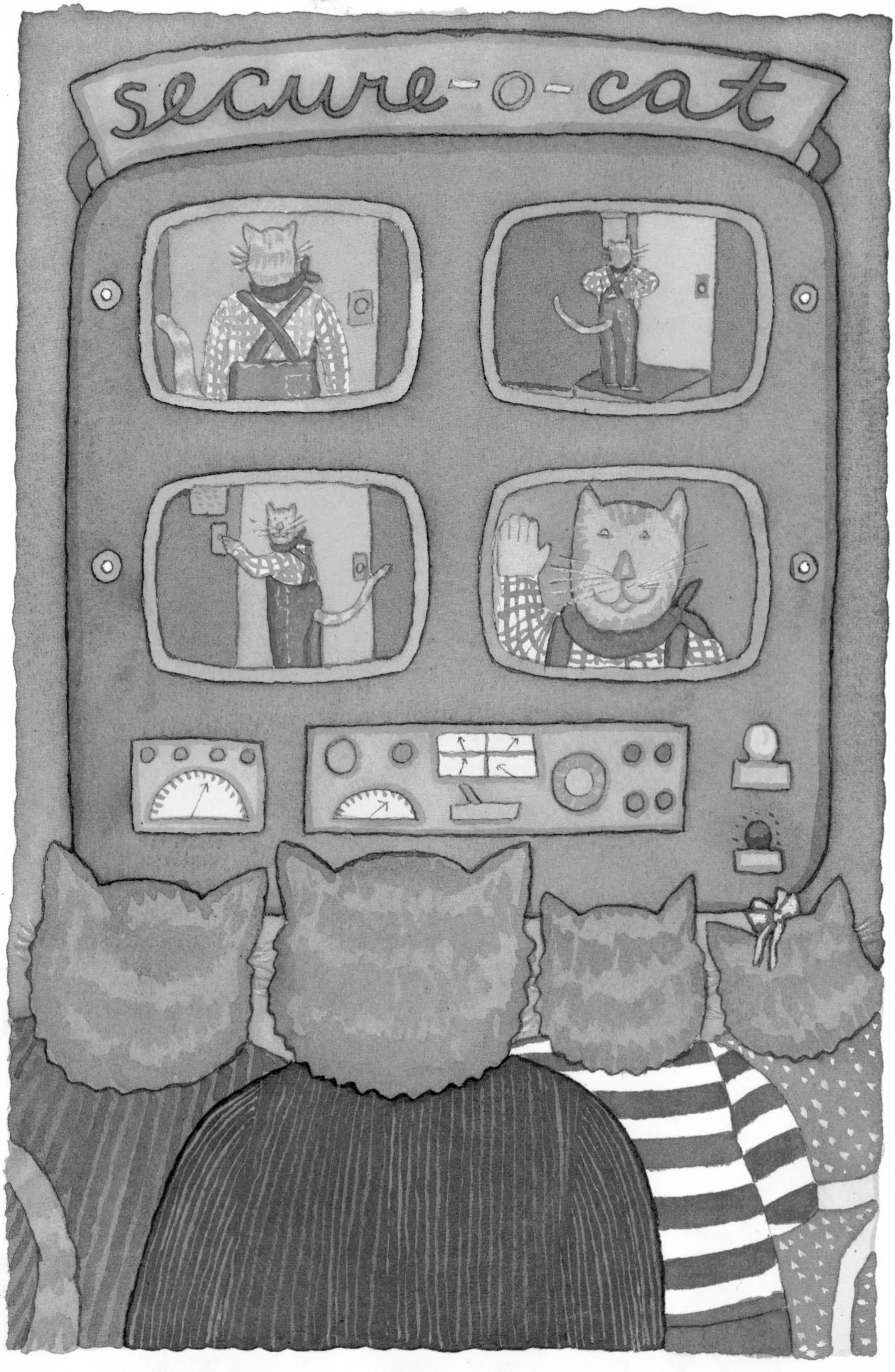
secure-o-cat

Cousin Scraggs no sooner buzzed the
buzzer than his face flashed on the
video viewer.

"What a creep!" said Sis Cat.

"What a weirdo," said Son Cat.

"What shall we do?" asked Father Cat.

"What we must do," said Mother Cat,
who prided herself on family feeling.
"Blood is blood, and kith is kin.
He's our coz, so buzz him in."

The fat cats did, but not all the way in,
not until Cousin Scraggs was

debugged, bathed and given a brand-new
hermetically sealed set of sani-clothes.

   Afterwards, Cousin Scraggs was given the
grand tour. He saw and tried out everything.
   He pushed all the buttons, created his
own concoctions, admired himself from all
angles and electronically obliterated
108, 737, 404½ Pack Rats.
   Cousin Scraggs had a wonderful time,
for a time.

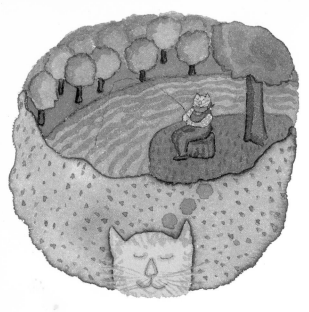

But after a while, he began to long
for the wind in his whiskers, the sun
on his back and the friendly familiarity
of fleas.

He began to grow tired of too-soft food,
a too-soft bed and a too-soft life.

And he began to grow fat.

It was then Cousin Scraggs decided
it was time to go.

He left after thanking his fat cat cousins
and shedding his sani-clothes.
    He no sooner left than he had a strange
uneasy feeling in the pit of his stomach.
    Something was wrong. Very wrong.

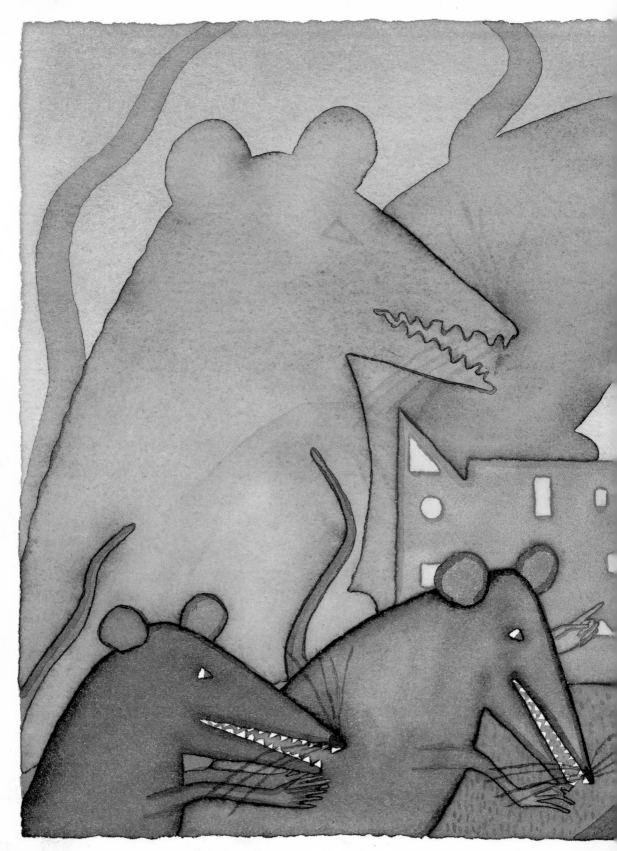

Large, looming shadows blotted out the sun.

Loud munching, crunching sounds hurt his ears.

Cousin Scraggs saw what was wrong as soon
as as his eyes adjusted to the dark.

The shadows were made by huge monster
mice, the same mean-looking mice who had
been drinking the pond. Only bigger.
Much bigger. The chemical purée in the
pond had made them into monsters.

And the loud munching, crunching sounds
came from the monster mice now chewing
and chomping the very foundation of the
fat cats' house.

Something had to be done. Cousin Scraggs debated what.

His first thought was to save himself.

His second thought was to try to save his cousins, too. His second thought won by a whisker.

Quickly Cousin Scraggs pussyfooted back to the front door. He buzzed the buzzer.

"Help!" he called into the intercom. "I forgot something important. Let me in."

Cousin Scraggs face once again flashed
on the video viewer. So did the faces of
a dozen monster mice, close behind and
gaining.

The fat cats buzzed their cousin in
just in the nick of time.

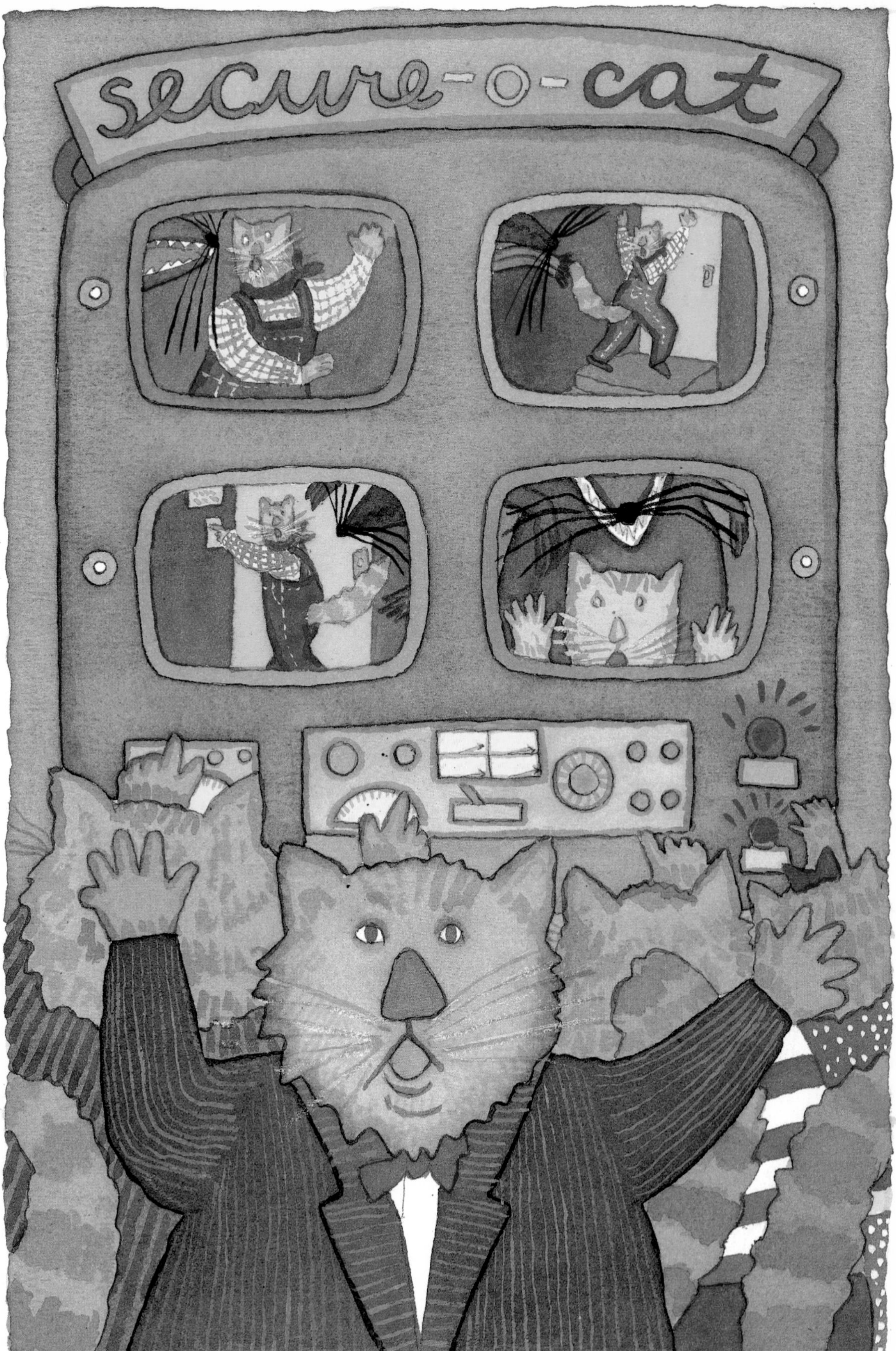
secure-o-cat

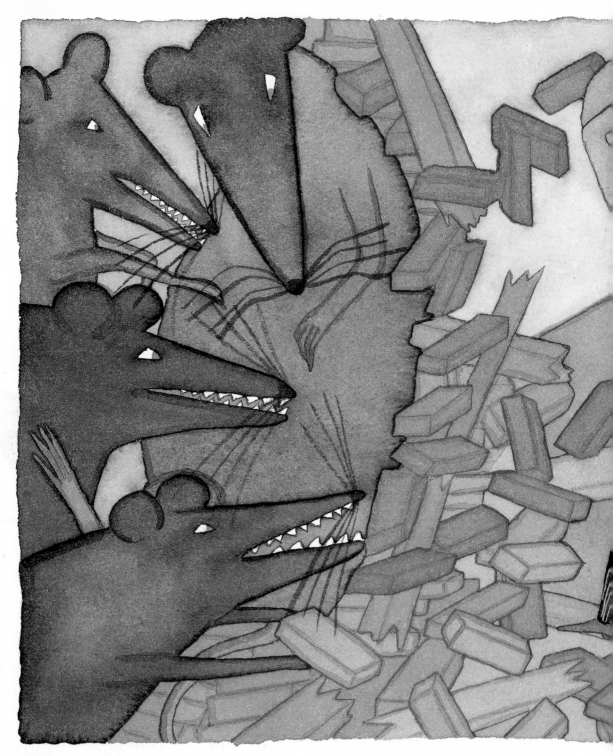

"What I forgot to tell you," said Cousin Scraggs,
"was about the big mean-looking mice who have been
drinking your pond. They've drunk it all up.
And they're still hungry. And now they're about
to eat the house down.

"We've got to get out of here. Fast!
Follow me!"

No one moved. Not until Cousin Scraggs
yelled, "NOW!" above the ear-splitting
avalanche of the outer wall crumbling.

Terrified, the fat cats toddled and waddled
after Cousin Scraggs, just ahead of the first
wave of monster mice. They huffed and puffed
through a maze of corridors and clutter.

They each tried to grab something on
the way. But Cousin Scraggs warned,
"Don't take anything with you but your
wits and your whiskers."

They made it out the front door and
onto the terrace.
   There, the exhausted fat cats ran the rest
of the way down the long, sloping lawn, just as

the most monstrous mouse of all chomped
the main electric wire in two, causing the
house and everything in it, including all
the monster mice, to be blown to bits.

"Now what will we do?" wailed
the now-homeless fat cats.

"Learn to live by your wits and your
whiskers," said Cousin Scraggs. "And
rebuild differently."

At first, there was a lot of ouching and grouching.

But the fat cats finally learned how
to work together, how to find food,
and even how to have fun.

By the time they did, they had built
a small but cosy cottage.

In it, the now not-so-fat cats and
Cousin Scraggs lived in great closeness
if not comfort.

Now that they had nothing
to make them happy,

they made their own happiness.

DISCARD

Hazen, Barbara Shook

The Fat Cats, Cousin
Scraggs and the
monster mice

Property Of
Bound Brook Schools
LAFAYETTE SCHOOL

OCT 0 5 1992
95
NOV 5 1997

© THE BAKER & TAYLOR CO.